A VERY FURRY CHRISTMAS MYSTERY

CURLY BAY ANIMAL RESCUE COZY MYSTERY BOOK 8

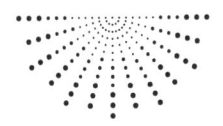

DONNA DOYLE

Publisher's Note: This is a work of fiction. Names, characters, places, and incidents are a product of the author's imagination. Locales and public names are sometimes used for atmospheric purposes. Any resemblance to actual people, living or dead, or to businesses, companies, events, institutions, or locales is completely coincidental.

© 2021 PUREREAD LTD

PUREREAD.COM

CONTENTS

Chapter 1	1
Chapter 2	10
Chapter 3	21
Chapter 4	34
Chapter 5	43
Chapter 6	50
Chapter 7	63
Chapter 8	72
Chapter 9	84
Chapter 10	99
Other books in this series	105
Our Gift To You	107

CHAPTER ONE

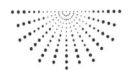

"Careful! You're really leaning over, Courtney!"

Reaching as far as her arm would go, Courtney hooked the last loop of garland around the top of the front lobby at the Curly Bay Pet Hotel and Rescue. She climbed back down the ladder to check out her work. Her lower back ached, and her feet hurt from climbing up and down the rungs of the ladder all day, but she'd made a lot of progress. "Looks pretty good, I guess. I think we could use a few more stars and bows, myself. And maybe a few more ornaments for the tree."

Dora shook her head and put her hand on her chest. "I think you're going to give me a heart attack if you don't stay off that ladder! You've got too much enthusiasm."

Courtney smiled at the groomer. "I just love Christmas, and I think it's important to put up all the decorations while we can. I've had a few years when I was too busy to bother until just a few days before, and then I just had to take it all back down again. It's not worth it if you can't leave it up for a few weeks and really enjoy it."

"We could've just put out the tabletop Christmas tree and called it good," Dora said as she stomped back off to the spa side of the business.

Courtney wasn't bothered. She knew Dora could be quite grumpy sometimes, and it was usually because something upset her. "Does she have a problem with the holidays?" she asked Ms. O'Donnell, who'd made a rare visit to the shelter to see how things were going.

"I think she just doesn't like the extra work," her boss replied, looking up and flicking her blonde hair back behind her shoulders. "She's very focused on those animals, as you know. I think she's addicted to clipping dog nails, sometimes, but to each their own. Now, what are we going to do to promote adoptions this holiday season? We're getting full again, and we need to make this a really big deal this year."

Courtney brought the empty decorations box back behind the counter and shut the little gate that separated the office area from the lobby. "I've been thinking about that quite a bit," Courtney said as she dusted off her hands and grabbed one of her notebooks to find the list she'd been making. It wasn't always easy to come up with new ideas for the same thing they were always trying to promote: adoptions. She'd worked in marketing before she'd come to Curly Bay, and she often found herself pulling out all the tricks she'd learned in the business. "We could dress them all up in little Santa and elf costumes and post pictures of them online along with what each pet wants for Christmas."

Ms. O'Donnell tapped her pen on her chin. "That's a good start, at least."

Courtney scanned her list. "I also thought about making an angel tree."

"What's that?"

"You put an ornament on the tree for each animal. On the back, we write what that animals needs for the holidays, like special food or a sweater. People can come in and sponsor a pet by taking an ornament and bringing back the supplies on the list. It isn't directly promoting adoptions, but it gives people a chance to help out and to think about the adoptees."

Ms. O'Donnell nodded. "Yes, and it won't cost us much of anything to make a few paper ornaments. I just wish there was a good way for us to really get out into the public eye. We had the booth and the parade during the Apple Jubilee, and those really got some adoptions going. Most of the Christmas events in Curly Bay are either indoors in places where we can't bring the pets, or they're outside where it's too cold." She curled her fist and rapped it gently on the corner of the counter. "This is a problem every year."

"Isn't there someplace that would make an exception for having the animals indoors?" Courtney asked. "Maybe I can talk to Lisa down at the library and see if they're doing anything."

"You're welcome to make all the phone calls you want, but I wouldn't get too hopeful if I were you," Ms. O'Donnell replied. "Most folks want to concentrate on other charities this time of year, like toy drives and food drives. Those are wonderful causes, of course, but it can put us in a real bind. That, and people often don't want to adopt a new pet when they're concerned about a cat climbing the

Christmas tree or a dog to deal with when they're trying to get out of town to visit relatives." She sighed again.

Courtney could tell her boss was getting very upset over this. The shelter was constantly looking for ways to either promote adoptions or fundraisers, and no matter how many dogs and cats they placed in new homes, there were always more. In that sense, it could be a frustrating job. "I'm sure we'll figure something out. We still have a little bit of time."

But Ms. O'Donnell wouldn't be consoled. She leaned forward and put her elbows on the counter. "There's never enough time in December. There are too many things to do. Even if I wasn't concerned about our current pet population here at the shelter, I'd still feel overwhelmed with all the shopping and wrapping and decorating. Then there are the parties. Don't get me wrong; I love Christmas. I just wish it wasn't so much work."

"Courtney! Courtney!" Jessi came barreling into the room. Her earrings today were Christmas trees made of twisted green wire that came down and brushed against her shoulders. She'd fully gotten into the holiday spirit with a rather garish sweater that also bore a tree on the front, and she held her phone up in the air. "Oh, good! You're here, Ms. O'Donnell. That means I can tell you both at once!"

The look of sheer joy on her face had Courtney intrigued. "What is it?"

Jessi pressed her lips together as her eyes widened even further. She looked like she was going to absolutely explode with excitement. "I just got off the phone with my older brother. He's a reporter for one of the big news stations in the city, but he'd interned here in Curly Bay at News 5 when he got his start. I'd been talking to him the other night and lamenting our usual problem of finding a way to encourage adoptions this time of year. Well, he happened to call me back this morning, and—Oh, I'm so excited!"

"What? What?" Ms. O'Donnell looked like she might burst at the seams, too.

"He talked to the station manager at News 5 and got us a spot to feature shelter pets on the evening news! You can bring in two animals tomorrow night to go live on the evening news!" Jessi clapped her hands and jumped up and down, making her earrings dance and bob all over again.

"Live?" Courtney asked, suddenly feeling a little faint.

"That's fantastic!" Ms. O'Donnell darted forward to wrap her arms around Jessi. "We've never had an opportunity like this before!"

"You'll probably want to go, since you're familiar with the station," Courtney said to Jessi.

But her employee shook her head. "No, you really ought to do it, Courtney. Besides, I'm terrified of being on camera. I'd just sit there and freeze, but you'll be great."

A queasy feeling was taking hold of Courtney's stomach. "And you say this is tomorrow night?" she asked weakly.

"Yep! The news starts at 6, but they want you to be there at least half an hour early so they can go over everything with you. Jason also said to make sure you don't wear anything with too much of a pattern on it. It won't translate well on TV, so no houndstooth or plaid."

"Jason?"

"Oh, that's my brother," Jesse replied.

"Right." Courtney had an odd feeling in the back of her throat. A soft head bumped up underneath her hand. It was Peppa, who'd come out of the office to comfort her owner. Courtney had started out being

Peppa's foster caregiver, bringing the beagle mix into her home so she'd have a place to stay when the shelter was bursting at the seams. The poor thing had been terrified of meeting anybody new, and shelter life really hadn't been working out for her. On Thanksgiving, however, Courtney had decided that she never wanted to think about Peppa going to live with someone else. Now, she took great comfort in the dog and Peppa's intuition about how she was feeling.

"Are you all right?" Ms. O'Donnell asked.

Courtney swallowed. "Sure. Yeah. I just don't want to take away the opportunity for someone else to go on TV if they want to. I mean, you're the owner, Ms. O'Donnell. Don't you want to do it?"

"I can't. I've got to go to my niece's birthday party tomorrow evening. But you're going to be great, Courtney. And don't worry. Everyone will be far more focused on the animals than they are on you."

Courtney certainly hoped so, but she wasn't entirely convinced.

Jessi's brow wrinkled. "I know this isn't easy, but Jason said this is the chance of a lifetime. Do you know how much it costs to put a commercial up, even on local TV? The shelter could never afford it, and they're giving this to us for free. It's a really big deal."

"I know. I know. And it'll be fine. Maybe we should just take a second to walk through and figure out which animals I should bring, shall we?" She gestured toward the shelter side of the building, happy to shift the focus off of herself but still a nervous wreck inside. Courtney had never been on television before, and she wasn't sure she wanted to be.

CHAPTER TWO

"All right, ladies. I expect you to be on your absolute best behavior. You were chosen because you're beautiful and charismatic, and we think you'll be perfect tonight. This could be the performance of your lifetime. No pressure, though, right?"

Flora and Autumn looked at Courtney expectantly from the back seat. Courtney, Ms. O'Donnell, and Jessi had all agreed that they'd be the best choices for the TV spot. Flora was a gorgeous Staffordshire mix, mostly white with a little bit of brown on her ears. She had a beautiful face and a sweet disposition. The chow mix Autumn was nothing but deep auburn fluff, and she had a ton of personality.

"And please understand that I'm beyond nervous," Courtney continued as she pulled into a parking spot at the station. "I hardly slept at all last night, so I'll probably have big old bags under my eyes. I haven't been able to eat anything beyond toast and crackers because my stomach keeps rolling around inside me. I'm just so glad to be getting this over with."

She got out of the car and got the dogs out of the back, hoping her own nerves didn't translate to the dogs. Animals can pick up on how a person is feeling, and Courtney didn't want their empathic abilities to ruin their chances of being seen on TV. Someone out there might happen to fall in love with one of them and call the shelter the next day, asking for an application. At least, that was what Courtney hoped for. These sweet girls definitely deserved homes for the holidays.

After checking in at the front desk, Courtney was brought back into the television studio itself. She'd had an idea of what it would look like based off what she'd seen on TV, but it was overwhelming to see it in real life. The floor was a snaky mess of cables that darted off in every direction, and yet people moved over them without even watching their feet. The news desk hadn't been lit up yet, but Courtney recognized it as the same one she saw on TV every night when she had dinner at home. Some windowed offices sat off to the left, and stacks of equipment were everywhere.

"Are you Chloe?" a gruff voice asked.

Courtney turned to see a man in his mid-forties glaring at her. His upper back was slightly stooped, and his graying hair was getting a little long around the ears. If Courtney felt her own eyes were baggy from a lack of sleep, it was nothing compared to the luggage this man carried. The front of his jeans had dirt ground into them. "Um, I'm Courtney, actually."

"Oh. I thought you were the woman from the shelter," he replied.

"I am. I'm Courtney Cain, from the Curly Bay Pet Hotel and Rescue," she specified, just in case they were expecting someone from another shelter somewhere. "I'm not sure who I need to talk to, but I guess I'm supposed to be on the news this evening?"

"Yeah, yeah. That's you, then," the man said with a roll of his eyes. "I'm Charlie Moss, and I'm the head cameraman around here. I'm supposed to show you around before things get started."

"I'd appreciate that." Courtney wasn't sure how much she really needed to know beyond where to sit and where to look, but it would be nice to get a feel for the place.

"I don't. The intern is supposed to do that, but he's out sick. I think he's faking it while he's out on a job interview, but it's not like anyone will believe me."

The mention of an intern jogged Courtney's memory. "My friend's brother interned here a while back. Maybe you know him. Jason Cooke?"

Charlie flicked a hand impatiently in the air. "Maybe. I don't know. The interns come and go, and I don't really bother to learn their names. Anyway, make sure you watch your step. I don't need any of these cables to be pulled out of place or tangled. It might look like a mess to you, but it's my mess, and I know where everything is." He stepped through the loops of cords with confidence.

"All right." Courtney would do her best, but she certainly couldn't guarantee that the dogs could get through without getting tangled in something.

"Over here, obviously, is the news desk," Charlie continued. "When it's time, someone will direct you to sit right here in this chair. Reese will talk to you for a bit about the dogs, and when she's done you'll hear the cut to commercial. That's when you can leave."

A couple cameramen came in to check over the equipment, and Courtney noticed they didn't say a word to Charlie as they went about their business.

He stomped over to a table loaded down with food. "This is the break area. You can help yourself, but don't get anything on you before you start. People will notice if you have a crumb on your shirt.

Just then, a beautiful young woman came into the studio. Though she wore high heels with her skirt suit, she maneuvered through the obstacle course on the floor with ease as she came over to them. "Is this our guest for the evening?" she asked brightly.

"You're Reese Riley." Courtney couldn't help the silly grin that came over here face at seeing the familiar anchorwoman. She was just a local newscaster, but Courtney still felt as though she was meeting a celebrity. "It's so nice to meet you."

"You, too, and I can't wait to get started on the story. Tell me about these two." She gestured at Fiona and Autumn.

"Huh! I guess you'll do anything to be on television, Riley. Doing a news story about dogs. That's not news." Charlie stormed off toward the cameras.

Reese bent to pet each of the dogs, careful not to crease her suit. "Don't mind him," she whispered. "He's always crabby like that. He thinks our broadcast should be all about the hard news, but there just isn't that much of it in Curly Bay."

Courtney believed that, especially since she'd lived in a much larger city before she'd moved here. "I really appreciate you having us on, but I'm a bit nervous."

Reese shook her head of perfectly sprayed blonde hair and smiled. "There's not a thing to be nervous about! You just relax and be yourself. That'll create the best performance."

"But, the cameras…" Courtney tried to explain. She'd hardly been able to even glance at the side of them so far.

"They stay far back, so they won't be in your face. Most of the time, you can just be looking at me or at the dogs. Just focus on how much you care about the dogs and finding them a home, and you'll be fine." Reese checked the big clock on the wall. "I'd better get in place. Someone will let you know when it's time to get on the set." She trotted off behind the desk.

A few minutes later, a heavyset man with beads of sweat running down his temple stopped by. He had a woman a little older than Courtney with him. "Hi, I'm Gordon Holder, the station manager. This is Kate Adams, our charity organizer. I take it you've already seen around the place a little?"

"Yes, thank you."

"Good, good. I'll let you know when it's time, and you just be yourself. It'll be over with before you know it. I'd be sure to keep an eye on the phone tomorrow, too. Everyone in town watches our program, and these pups will be the stars of the show."

"That'd be great." Courtney really was happy to think of Fiona and Autumn going to new homes, but she also knew this meant the time for her to go on camera was only coming closer.

Before she knew it, she was seated in the chair to the left of the news desk and Reese was introducing her. Courtney took one glance at the big lenses of the cameras and decided that the anchorwoman's advice was best. She'd stick to looking at Reese or the dogs.

"Today, we have Courtney Cain from the Curly Bay Pet Hotel and Rescue with us to talk about the cats and dogs who are looking for new homes this season. Courtney, tell us a little bit about who you've brought with you."

That was when both of the well-behaved canines she'd brought in decided to get a little nutty. Flora tried to hide under the chair, wrapping the leash around Courtney's hand. Autumn was stretching out to the end of her leash, sniffing the air for the food on the break table. She tried to get them under control as she spoke. "Flora here is feeling a bit shy, but she's a two-year-old Staffordshire mix who gets along well with kids and other pets. Autumn is a chow mix, and we believe she's around five. We know she gets along well with dogs and children, but not cats."

"I see. And could you tell us why you brought older dogs today instead of puppies?" Reese leaned forward with interest.

Courtney was indeed getting caught up enough in the dogs that she soon forgot she was talking to anybody but Reese. She managed to get Autumn to sit patiently at her side, and she coaxed Flora out from under the chair without too much trouble. "Puppies get all the attention at the shelter. They're little and cute, and it's rare that we hold onto them for long. People often forget about adult dogs, thinking they want something they can raise their entire lives. The truth is that adult dogs are absolutely wonderful, and you get to skip that puppy stage where they tend to tear everything up."

"Wonderful." Reese scratched Flora behind the ears and smiled. "What's your adoption process like?"

Without hardly even thinking about the words, Courtney launched into the paperwork and background checks that were required. This was information she spit out on a regular basis, and she didn't have to think about it at all.

"Do you have any recommendations for folks who are looking to adopt a pet this holiday season?"

"Yes. Adopting any animal at any time of year isn't something you want to do spontaneously. Make sure you understand all the responsibilities and costs. If you're not certain whether a pet will fit well into your family, we do offer home visits. This means a cat or dog can come stay with you for a week, but you can bring them back to the shelter if it doesn't work out."

Autumn flopped her head onto Courtney's knee and looked up at her with big, soulful eyes.

"Fantastic. If you're interested in adopting Flora or Autumn, or if you have any further questions, you'll find the website and phone number for the Curly Bay Pet Hotel and Rescue at the bottom of your screen. Thank you so much, Courtney."

"Thank you."

"And cut!" Charlie called.

Courtney's shoulders sagged, but she smiled. "That went a lot better than I thought it would. Thanks for the advice."

"You did great!" Reese enthused as she petted the dogs. "In fact, I was wondering if you might come back tomorrow with a couple of different dogs."

Courtney blinked. "Really?"

"Yes! These adorable little things are going to be fantastic for our ratings, not to mention my career," she laughed. "I'll have to double-check with Mr. Holder and Kate, but I think another spot would be a really good thing."

"Okay, sure," Courtney replied breathlessly. "Is it all right if I bring someone with me? That'll make them a little easier to handle." Though she'd gotten Flora and Autumn under control, Courtney had thought for a moment that her few minutes on TV might end up looking more like a comedy special.

"Sure! Not a problem!"

When Courtney left the station a few minutes later, after she and Reese had both checked in with Mr. Holder, she loaded the dogs into the car and gave them lots of love. "You girls were terrific! I can't wait to see all the calls and emails we get about you! You're stars!"

Flora licked Courtney's cheek and Autumn gave a small woof. Some people might say otherwise, but Courtney knew they understood they'd done a good job.

"Do you want to come to my house and have a sleepover with Peppa?" she asked. Courtney was ready to spoil them silly. They'd been a bit of a handful at first, but now that it was over she was grateful for how well it had gone. She headed home for a busy night of dogs playing on the living room floor.

CHAPTER THREE

"They're really getting the downtown area decorated for the season, aren't they?" Courtney leaned forward to peer through the windshield a little better. The lampposts along the main street had all been wrapped with garland and tied with bows. A big lighted sign stretched from one side of the street to the other, and there were Christmas trees in almost every show window.

"Oh, yeah," Jessi replied, holding Fishstick in her lap. The little dog was dressed in a festive Christmas sweater and seemed quite content to be going on a field trip. "They always go all out around here. The sense of community is one thing I really like about Curly Bay, and it really comes out at Christmas time."

"Ms. O'Donnell mentioned there were some municipal events. What do they have going on?" This was Courtney's first Christmas in Curly Bay, and it was already a far cry from what she'd experienced in the city. Yes, there'd been more options for shopping, but she was pretty sure she wouldn't miss it.

"Oh, there's tons of stuff. They have a few days where all the local stores are promoted for Christmas shopping, where they either offer special discounts or you get a prize if you get a card stamped by a certain number of them. They have a big drive-in movie event at the high school where the police hand out hot chocolate and cookies. There's a big event for the Christmas tree lighting event in the park. The park district hosts an Elves' Workshop night so kids can come in and make crafts or gifts. There's just tons of stuff, and that's not even all of it." Jessi took a sip from the travel mug of hot cocoa she'd brought with her.

"You sound like you really get into all of it," Courtney noted.

"Oh, yeah! As much as I can, anyway. I never seem to get everything done that I want to. I've barely even started my Christmas shopping."

Courtney nodded as she made the turn to head north toward the TV station. "I know. I've ordered a few things online, but I've got tons more yet to do. At least when we're done tonight, I should have my evenings back for a while. Not that I'm not grateful to your brother for this chance. We should send him a card or something."

Jessi grinned. "He said he watched you on the news last night and to tell you that you did well."

"I did not," Courtney said, her cheeks heating slightly. She didn't know Jessi's brother, but the idea of *anyone* seeing her on TV still embarrassed her. "Now I just have to figure out how to get you to stand in for me."

Wrapping her arms around Fishstick, Jessi shook her head firmly. "No way, José! I'll help you switch out the dogs as you talk about them, but that's it!"

"Why are you so scared of the camera?" Courtney didn't particularly enjoy it herself, and she knew she had zero plans of trying to become an actress, but she was still curious.

Jessi tipped her head to the side, making her snowflake earrings sparkle in the streetlamps. "You could blame it on my brother. He always had a camera out and going. Jason knew he wanted to be a reporter since he was a kid, you see, but he had to do all the reporting from behind the camera. I think what really did it, though, was when I was in the junior high play."

"But that's a play, not a TV studio," Courtney argued.

"Sure, but Jason was there with his camera. I was playing Mrs. Cratchit in *A Christmas Carol,* and my dress was too long. I tripped and fell right down the stage stairs, and Jason caught the whole thing. I was embarrassed enough that everybody was laughing, but then I had to watch it on video about a thousand times as my brother kept replaying it." Jessi hugged the dog a little tighter. "I told myself I'd never get behind the camera again."

That didn't quite sound like the same guy who'd gotten his little sister some help for the shelter. "You must've been really mad at him."

"Oh, sure, but I got over it. He was just a kid, too. I'm still not going on, though, if that's what you're getting at." Jessi gave her a grin.

They got out of the car and headed inside. Courtney knew how to navigate through the building to the correct studio now, but when they got there they found complete chaos. Charlie was standing in front of the cameras, waving his arms as he shouted at the other two cameramen. Mr. Holder had just marched out of his office to get involved. Kate Adams stood over by the food table, and Reese Riley examined her manicure while she waited for everything to calm down.

Courtney had brought in Scarlet, a lab mix, and the poor dog was clearly upset at seeing all this shouting. She cowered by Courtney's legs. "Um, let's just go over here and stay out of the way," she suggested, leading the way over to the food table. She'd put a few treats in her pockets, and she gave one to Scarlet to let her know she was being a good girl.

One went to Fishstick as well, who was cuddled up in Jessi's arms. "Is this what it was like last night?" Jessi whispered as they hovered in a corner. "I got to stop in a time or two when Jason was here, but I don't remember it being like this."

"It's new to me, but I'm no expert."

"The cable is bad," one cameraman said, shaking the offending cable in his hand. "It's not the camera at all."

"I thought that cable was supposed to be replaced last week," another cameraman commented. "Charlie said he'd take care of it!"

Charlie put his hands in the air. "Hey, now! I'd have a lot more time to take care of things around here if you two weren't always goofing off! I'm the only one who actually does any work. You two just think you can point the camera at a pretty face and doze off for an hour. When was the last time you actually paid attention to your framing? I'd guess never!"

"All right, all right!" Mr. Holder shouted. "This has gone on long enough. Let's get that cable replaced, and pronto. Then that just leaves us with the lighting issue."

The cameraman who held the bad cable motioned vaguely toward Charlie. "Someone was supposed to order more lightbulbs, but…"

Pandemonium ensued once again as everyone argued over who to blame for a lack of bulbs.

"I don't care who's responsible," Mr. Holder bellowed. "I just want it done!"

Courtney watched it all with interest, but she also wished it would be over with soon. The arguments were really scaring poor Scarlet. Courtney knelt down and stroked her ears, telling her what a good girl she was.

Meanwhile, a young man with a headset came out of the control booth and approached Kate. "I guess they haven't sorted this mess out yet?"

Kate rolled her eyes. "No, and I'm starting to wonder if they'll be arguing about it until the new year."

"They're not arguing with you. Why do you look so sour?" the young man asked.

Kate flicked her fingers toward the anchorwoman across the room. "We've got another spot on tonight with the pet shelter."

"Right. You should be happy about that, since you're the one in charge of making sure the station sponsors local charities," he pointed out.

"Yes, but Reese is going to take all the credit for it. You haven't been in the business long enough to know that the people behind the scenes are always the ones who get the shaft, while those in front of the camera get all the fame and the credit. People don't see me making phone calls and coordinating schedules. They see her petting puppies."

Courtney exchanged a look with Jessi. Either Kate didn't realize they were standing there, or she didn't care.

"I don't think you need to worry about that," the man said. "It's not like she went and pulled the dogs out of a burning building. She doesn't do anything but read what's on the prompter."

"Just you wait and see," Kate advised. "And to top it all off, we've got the most conceited cameraman in the world locking up our broadcast. What a day!"

Courtney continued to comfort Scarlet as she thought about this. Jason was the one who'd arranged for them to be at News 5, but he must've had to coordinate that *with* someone. Was that Kate? Or did he have other connections, like perhaps Reese Riley? The anchorwoman had at least been the one who set up tonight's guest spot, even if she hadn't scheduled last night's. Courtney hoped she wasn't doing anything to fuel the feud that seemed to be going on among the staff here.

The lights came on over the news desk as Mr. Holder started yelling once again. "All right, everyone! Get to your places! We've only got a few minutes, and I won't tolerate us going on the air even a second late!" He glared at Charlie as he headed toward the control booth.

Soon enough, Courtney once again got lost in the idea of being interviewed by Reese. She held Fishstick on her lap while she discussed senior dogs and how hard shelter life was on them. A quick trade with Jessi and she had Scarlet sitting in front of her, looking around anxiously but wagging her tail and behaving. It went smoothly and quickly, and Reese had managed to come up with new questions for her this time.

"I read on your website that you have a foster program. Can you tell us a little bit more about that?"

Courtney brightened. She'd thought the focus would be entirely on the pets they'd brought in, but Reese seemed happy to talk about anything related to the shelter. This was a great chance to really get a lot of information out there. "Our foster program was started recently due to not having enough space at the shelter," Courtney said with a smile. "We've been really pleased with the amount of people here in Curly Bay who've come forward to help care for these homeless pets. The process is very similar to that of adopting, but we still take care of all the vet fees."

"Do people ever decide to adopt their foster pets?" Reese asked.

Courtney had to laugh. "Guilty as charged! I've already done it myself, and we've had quite a few others do the same. Sometimes you really get attached, and it's hard to let go."

"It's hard for me to imagine why anyone would want to let go of this beautiful girl," Reese replied as she reached out her hand to let Scarlet sniff it. "Thank you so much for coming in today, Courtney. If you'd like to find out more information about the Curly Bay Pet Hotel and Rescue or to adopt these adorable dogs, call the number on your screen or visit their website. We'll be right back."

Once again, Courtney felt the snap back to reality. It was like a collective breath was let out when everyone returned to their normal selves during the commercial break. She petted Scarlet on her head and worked her way back over to Jessi, but a hand wrapped around her arm.

"Courtney! I wanted to talk to you about another idea!" Reese was just as perfect today as she'd been the night before. This time she wore gray slacks with a sweater, and not a hair was out of place.

"All right."

Reese pressed her fingertips together in front of her. "We've had some of the adoptable pets on the air, but what if we talked to the other *people* behind the story? I'm talking about folks who've adopted pets, or fostered them, or even people who might come volunteer at the shelter. Of course they can bring their dogs or cats, as well, but I think it would be a great way to help get the word out there. Folks at home would see that this isn't just a about pets who need a home, but also about how it affects people. You know what I mean?"

"I do, but that sounds like a much longer spot on the news," Courtney hedged. "Are you sure you'd have time for that?"

Reese waved a hand in the air. "It would be fine! We need something to fill up our airtime besides community events and weather. Even the national news only takes up so much. What do you say?"

Courtney opened her mouth and closed it again. The last couple of spots had gone well despite her worst fears, and she knew just how fortunate they were to have this time. "I'll need a day or two to arrange some people. I don't know who might be available."

"You'll find plenty of them!" Reese enthused. "I can hardly keep them from coming around behind me when I get to do the news remotely, with everyone jumping and yelling in the background. I'm sure you won't have anything to worry about."

"Okay. Can I get back in touch when I have things lined up?"

"Just call the station, and they'll patch you through," Reese assured her before heading off to her dressing room.

"Oh, great," Charlie grumbled nearby. "More dog stories. Just the kind of hard journalism people want to see."

"Well, that was all a bit different than I imagined," Jessi said as they headed out to the car a few minutes later.

"I really appreciate you coming with me," Courtney replied as she loaded Scarlet into the back. "It was so much easier not to have to handle both dogs at once."

Jessi snuggled Fishstick close. "We probably won't be handling either one of them for long. After all the calls we got today about Flora and Autumn, I imagine these two will be home for the holidays before we know it."

Courtney started the engine and put on her seatbelt, smiling. "Yeah, the place was really going crazy. This is going to be one of the best promotions we've ever had."

CHAPTER FOUR

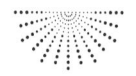

"I'm starting to feel like I live at the TV station," Courtney said the next night as she yet again headed across town. "It's really good for the shelter, and we've had so many calls and emails that we can hardly keep up with them. I never thought a rescue would need holiday help, but I'm starting to think I might need to hire someone temporarily. Either that, or I'll just have to start pulling double shifts."

"I've been watching the spots, and I think you're doing great," Lisa said from the passenger seat. Lisa Patterson was as new to Curly Bay as Courtney was, and the two of them were becoming good friends. Her own foster-turned-adopted dog Beau was in the back seat, and her cat Sage was curled up on her lap wearing his harness and leash. Lisa had instantly agreed to come on the news, so Courtney hadn't had any delay in getting back to Reese. "I don't know how I'll do in front of the camera."

"You'll do fine. On the first night, Reese told me to just focus on her and the pets like we were having a personal conversation. I don't know what I would've done without that advice. It really helped keep me from obsessing over the camera too much. Not that I want this to become my career, by any means."

"I wouldn't want to, either, but it's great that this has been so good for the shelter. Maybe once you're done with the news spots, we can find some other ways for you to feature the animals. I know you post a lot to social media, but obviously these gigs are having a really big impact."

"Do you have any ideas?" Courtney asked. Lisa had a full-time job down at the Curly Bay Library, but she volunteered as much of her time helping out the shelter as possible. She was always full of good ideas.

"Nothing specific, yet. I'm sure there's something we can come up with, though."

Shana Pitkin met them in the parking lot, and she took a carrier covered in a warm blanket from the back of her car as they pulled up.

"How are all the babies doing?" Courtney asked, peeking through the blanket at the five little faces inside.

"They're a mess!" Shana laughed. "They've been mobile and curious for quite some time, but now they're literally climbing the walls."

"Sounds like they're about ready for some new homes," Courtney said as that same warm feeling that she always felt when she heard a successful story come over her. Shana had agreed to foster Petunia, an expecting mother cat who'd come to the shelter. Since Shana worked from home, she was the perfect person to keep an eye on her. "And how about mama?"

"Actually, I wanted to talk to you about Petunia," Shana began as they walked inside.

Alarm bells went off in Courtney's mind. "Is she all right?"

"Oh, she's fine. Better than fine, actually. She likes to sprawl out on my desk while I'm working. I thought maybe that was just to get some time away from her brood, but I'm starting to think she likes me as much as I like her. I'd like to adopt her."

"Shana! That's fantastic! You're going to make me cry!" Courtney put an arm around the foster parent. "I never have any doubt that the kittens are going to find homes, since they're so cute and little, but I always worry about the mothers. That would be wonderful!"

"Don't take me off the foster list, though," Shana replied. "I absolutely loved being there for Petunia and her babies, and I want to do it again in the future if you get another pregnant cat in."

The studio wasn't nearly as chaotic as it'd been last night, but Courtney sensed some tension as soon as they walked in. Reese was sitting at her spot behind the news desk, but she was glaring at the monitors that showed her image. "Charlie, you've got to fix the lighting."

"I already did," he groused.

"No. Or if you did, then you overcorrected. Now I'm too washed out." She tipped her face one way and then the other as she studied the monitor.

The cameraman checked the image and flicked a few switches. "There. Is that better?"

Reese's frown deepened. "Are you even looking at it? You overcorrected again, and now my face is all shadowed."

"You're too picky. Nobody really cares about what you look like. They just want to hear the news."

"Clearly you have no idea what it means to be on this side of the lens," Reese retorted. "It might sound shallow to you, but it's not like anyone wants me sitting here in my bathrobe. It has to be right. Now do your job and fix it!" She muttered something about the staff holding back her career as she picked up a stack of papers next to her and began studying them.

"Sorry about that," Courtney muttered as they headed over to the side of the room to wait. "It seems there's always some sort of drama going on here."

The broadcast began, and Courtney and her guests waited patiently. They'd just finished with the weather and taken a commercial break when Mr. Holder came bursting out of the control room. "There's a big fire downtown. I've already got a reporter there, but he's just got a cell phone. I need a camera operator post haste!"

"I'll go!" said a young man eagerly.

"You will not!" Charlie snapped. "I'm the head operator here, and if there's any actual news going on, then I should be the one to film it." He marched over to a shelf against the wall and took down a portable camera in a case. "All you young'uns need to get your technical skills down before you can take a job like this one."

Everyone watched him leave without a word, and Mr. Holder returned to the control room. The two remaining cameramen, however, weren't happy.

"How do you like that?" the young man who'd originally volunteered said. "There goes Charlie, doing whatever he wants, and not a word gets said about it."

The second guy shrugged. "Not a surprise, though, right? We're on in ten."

They scrambled to their positions, and the news started up once again. It was soon time for their spot, and Courtney was grateful she wasn't the one being interviewed tonight. She got to stand back and watch as Lisa talked about Beau, her border collie mix. He was a sweet boy, but the real story was in the little gray kitten who'd fallen in the love with him. Courtney remembered how concerned she'd been when the cat kept disappearing, but she always found him over in the kennel with Beau. The two of them were the best of friends, and Lisa had decided to adopt them both.

Next came Shana, who was a natural in front of the camera, even with an armload of kittens. Her cheeks flushed slightly as she talked about what it was like to help guide Petunia into motherhood, and how wonderfully distracting the kittens were to her work.

"Can I hold one?" Reese asked.

"Absolutely!" Shana handed over a little orange and white puffball. "This is Carrot."

"Hi, Carrot!" Reese had mentioned to Courtney how good the animals were for her career, but she saw sheer joy in the anchorwoman's face as the snuggled the little kitten close. "You're a sweet thing, aren't you?"

The kitten touched his nose to the tip of hers.

When Reese finished up, thanked Shana, and cut to commercial, she was still holding Carrot when Courtney came over to help Shana get all the kittens back in their carrier. "This was a wonderful segment!" she bubbled as she rubbed her chin against Carrot's fuzzy head. "You picked the perfect people to come in, Courtney. I hope this helps out your foster program."

"I have no doubt it will," Courtney assured her. "We've been getting calls nonstop after the last two nights."

"So let's make things even bigger and better," Reese suggested as she scratched her manicured nails against Carrot's coat. The kitten closed his eyes and purred. "How about I bring a camera crew down to the shelter?"

"Really?" Courtney asked. She'd finally gotten used to the coming to the station, and now she felt nervous all over again. "You'd want to do that?"

"Yes! It would be a pre-recorded spot, so it wouldn't have to be during the evening. It would give us a great chance to go through and show a whole bunch of the available animals, instead of just one or two." She tucked Carrot into the crook of her arm, paying no attention to the fur that clung to her suit jacket as she tickled his belly.

"I'd have to check with the owner to see if it's okay. And we might need a little time to prepare," Courtney hedged. She didn't think Ms. O'Donnell would have a problem with it, especially if it meant more adoptions, but she still wasn't going to agree to anything that big without her permission.

"Of course! And we can even talk about the hotel and day spa side of things, too. I saw that it helps fund the shelter, so it's relevant. It'll be a big segment, but I can make it work. Can't I, darling?" she cooed at Carrot.

"All right. I'll discuss it and let you know as soon as possible."

"Thirty seconds!" called out one of the cameramen.

"All right." Reese held the kitten in her hands, looking into his little face. "You're the most handsome man I ever met, you know that? You go back to your home for now, but maybe I'll see you again soon." She handed Carrot back to Shana.

CHAPTER FIVE

Ms. O'Donnell took a compact out of her desk and checked her reflection, adjusting her necklace and her hair. "What time are they supposed to be here?"

"Reese is arriving early. She said she wants to have a look around before they get started, so she should be here around one o'clock. Then the rest of the crew is coming around two." Courtney picked up one of her numerous notebooks and checked her list.

"And we're all ready to go?" Ms. O'Donnell asked.

"Almost everything is crossed off the list," Courtney assured her. "Everyone has had a fresh grooming, and we've practically gone over the cages and kennels with a toothbrush. All the floors are mopped, and I changed out the lightbulb in the hallways. If anyone finds anything wrong with this place when they get here, then they're too picky."

Ms. O'Donnell closed her compact with a click. "I'm sure you're right. And don't take all my fussing as me thinking you're not capable of running this place. It always looks wonderful. I just know that sometimes the camera picks up things that we don't see with our own eyes, and I'd hate to find a mistake later. This is worse than having in-laws over for Christmas dinner."

"Don't worry. I'm sure everything will be fine. And there's no doubt it's had a good effect on us," Courtney said as the phone rang yet again. She heard Dora pick it up over in the grooming salon.

The anchorwoman showed up just a few minutes later, beaming from ear to ear as always. "Hi, Courtney! Hi, Jessi! Oh, this place is great! It's so nice and clean in here. I've been to a few shelters before, and they're not usually like this."

"We do our best," Courtney said. "This is Melanie O'Donnell, the owner of Curly Bay Pet Hotel and Rescue. Ms. O'Donnell, this is Reese Riley."

The two women shook hands, and Ms. O'Donnell actually looked nervous. "It's so very nice to meet you, and I can't tell you how much I appreciate all you're doing to help our mission. What can we do to get you started?"

"I'd just like to take a look around, check out the background, and make sure I know where I'm going so I look comfortable on camera. Is Carrot here today?"

Courtney shook her head. "I'm afraid not. He and his siblings are staying with Shana for a little bit longer. We don't have a lot of space at the moment, so they'll probably go straight from her place to their forever homes."

Reese stuck out her bottom lip in a pout. "Well, that's okay. Let's see what else you've got."

Courtney escorted her into the cat room, where Reese peered into every cage and looked at all the name tags. She turned around and took a selfie with her back to the cages, checking the image in her phone and nodding. She seemed completely absorbed in what she was doing as she scrutinized the color of her outfit against the walls, and she even took a small light meter out of her pocket to check the illumination in the room.

When they moved to the kennel, Reese's eyes widened at all the barking. "Oh. It's going to be hard to shoot in here. Do they always bark like that?"

Courtney lifted her shoulders. "Pretty much, especially if someone new is in the room. They don't bark at any of us, really, but if you or the camera crew are in here, this is probably what it's going to be like."

Reese frowned and nodded. "Okay. I'll have Charlie do a sweeping shot of the kennels so we can see everyone, but we'll dub it over with my voice. I want to showcase as many of the dogs as possible, though, so maybe we can bring one or two of them out into the main area?"

"Of course."

"Let's get this guy here out. He seems cute. I want to see how he'll be with me, though." Reese took several more selfies with several dogs, experimenting with sitting on the floor with them versus sitting in a chair or even holding them.

Courtney hadn't realized that Reese would be so willing to get hands-on. She'd expected a simple walk-through while the reporter asked a few questions, but Reese was treating this like an art form that she'd studied for a long time. She wanted all the best angles and exposures, and it almost made Courtney wonder why *she* wasn't the one behind the camera.

"Where is that man?" Reese muttered as she checked her watch an hour later. "He should be here by now."

"I don't see anybody," Courtney said as she glanced out in the parking lot. "Maybe he's just running a few minutes late. No worries, though. We're not on a super tight schedule today."

But Reese was already dialing on her cell. "He claims to be a professional, and he's always whining about how he should be working for a bigger station. He ought to know that if he isn't early, then he's late. That's how you miss the big stories, you know." She tapped the toe of her bright pink pump impatiently while she listened to it ring. "He's not answering."

"Maybe he's driving?" Courtney offered. She knew that Reese and Charlie didn't get along. As a matter of fact, it didn't seem that anybody down at News 5 got along. Still, she didn't want the kind of arguments she often saw in the studio to come along with them to the shelter. "I'm sure he'll be here any minute."

After several more phone calls, though, there was still no sign of Charlie. "That's it. I'm calling Mr. Holder. Not that he's going to do anything about it but make excuses. I'll go as high as I can if that's what it takes, and maybe after that I'll just go off and look for a job at one of the other stations!" Reese dialed angrily.

Courtney stepped back toward the counter in the lobby, feeling awkward. Was it really worth it to have all these TV spots if they were going to be so much trouble? What if Charlie showed up, and he and Reese had a big blowout? Sure, they weren't going live, so that sort of thing didn't need to be on camera, but Courtney didn't want the animals disturbed. Shelter life was hard enough on them as it was.

"What the heck? He's not answering, either!" Reese redialed, fuming. She turned toward Courtney. "I'm so sorry about this. This isn't how it's supposed to be. Nothing has been over the past few weeks, to be honest with you. It's one thing if it's behind the scenes, but it's another when—Ed! There you are!" She turned toward the front doors as the other end of the line was picked up. "I've been trying to call you. I can't seem to reach anybody today, and I've got a shoot scheduled over here at the shelter. We talked about this, you know, and—what? What do you mean, it isn't going to happen today? Just send someone else!" Reese's face changed as she listened, turning from anger and frustration to concern and maybe even shock. "I understand. Yes. Yes, I'll do that. Thank you, Ed."

The reporter hung up and pocketed her phone. Her shoulders and back had gone stiff, and even with all her makeup she looked a little pale as she turned to Courtney. "Um, I'm afraid we're not going to be able to do this today," she said quietly.

"That's perfectly all right." Courtney hated to waste the time they'd spent preparing, but it was obvious this was more than just a scheduling error. Had Reese gotten fired or something? "Can I ask what's wrong?"

Reese nodded and swallowed, but she didn't answer right away. She took her cell back out of her pocket, looked at it, and put it away again. "It seems that Charlie isn't going to be able to make it. He's dead."

CHAPTER SIX

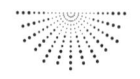

T he air was cool and crisp, but it wasn't yet into the coldest part of the year. Courtney knew that would come around January or February, according to what all the locals said. That was when the snow and possibly even ice storms would really start, but for now there was a distinctive winter chill as Courtney dressed Peppa in an insulated vest and dog boots. "You be a good girl tonight, okay? If you're chilly, we'll come home early." She'd debated quite a bit on whether or not to bring Peppa along with her that evening, but she'd decided she couldn't just leave her at home. She'd been spending her evenings with the other dogs from the shelter, and the guilt was starting to weigh on her.

"You made it!" Lisa said when Courtney found her near the hot chocolate stand. "This will be the first Curly Bay Christmas tree lighting for both of us!"

Beau and Peppa greeted each other with wagging tails. Beau was dressed for the weather as well, including a jaunty little Santa hat over his ears.

"I'm excited about it. All my time has been spent on the shelter lately. You know I don't mind, but I definitely didn't want to miss this. There are so many people here, and I wasn't sure I was going to find a place to park. Oh, there's Nathan!" She waved at her neighbor, who saw her and headed in their direction.

Nathan Park was Courtney's neighbor as well as a web developer who sometimes did volunteer work on the Curly Bay Pet Hotel and Rescue's website. He was also the proud owner of a big fat marmalade named Archie. "Hi, ladies. It's good to see you here."

"I'm starting to think everyone I know is here," Courtney commented as she looked around, recognizing people she knew from the shelter, the store, and even the post office.

"It's a great event. You'll see. I caught each of you on the news, by the way. You did a great job."

Courtney was ready to talk about it in more detail, but a trumpet sounded from the other side of the park as Mayor Bridget Powers stepped up to a podium. "Ladies and gentlemen, we're just about ready to start. I first want to thank you all for coming out in support of Curly Bay. Events like this remind me every year of what a great community we have, and there are so many volunteers who made it all come together."

As the mayor went through a list of everyone who'd helped, Courtney scanned the crowd. She saw the owners of her favorite restaurants, Eric who worked down at the office supply store, and the wealthy Mrs. Throgmorton. No matter what sort of background, it seemed that everyone in Curly Bay had turned up for this event. She had to wonder if Charlie Moss was the type who would've been here. He certainly hadn't seemed like much of a people person.

The high school band broke out into a beautiful rendition of 'O, Christmas Tree' while candles were passed out. Courtney hadn't expected this. "I don't have any matches or anything," she said.

"Don't worry about it," Nathan said from next to her. "Look."

Courtney peered through the crowd to see that candles were being lit all through the park. Those few who had brought matches or a lighter used their candles to light the flames of their neighbors'. Complete strangers turned to those next to them, making sure they could continue the spread of Christmas cheer through an act as simple as lighting a candle. Someone offered to light Nathan's candle with their own, he in turn lit Courtney's, and she lit Lisa's as they passed it on. It was one of the most beautiful things Courtney had ever witnessed.

Her mind was changed a moment later when Mayor Powers got on the mic once again. "All right, folks. It's the moment you've all been waiting for! Let's do a countdown. Ten…nine…eight…"

The whole town chanted together until the tree was lit, and it brought tears to Courtney's eyes as applause rang out through the night sky. It was just a tree, and it wasn't as though she hadn't seen a million of them, but it was completely different from anything she'd done in the city. This tree really meant something to the people of Curly Bay, and the fact that they were all standing out here with their breath fogging the air proved it.

"That was wonderful," she said when the mayor stepped down from her podium.

"That's not even all of it," Nathan said. "They've got a little Santa hut set up down there where children can go in for free photos. If you head up there at the northeast corner of the park, you can get a ticket for a sleigh ride. It's really a wagon ride, but that's the best we can do without any horses. Over behind us there's a booth selling souvenirs. One of my friends is running it, and I promised I'd help him out. You should stop over there and see us."

"We will," Courtney promised. "Thanks."

Lisa nudged her with her elbow when Nathan had gone. "I think he wanted *you* to stop over there and see him."

"Oh, I don't know about that." Courtney glanced over her shoulder at where Nathan had joined his friend under a marquee boasting t-shirts, mugs, and ornaments that said, 'Curly Bay Annual Christmas Tree Lighting.' He was a handsome man, and she got along well with him. He was an animal person, and he volunteered his time for the shelter.

"I hope this isn't about Sam Smythe," Lisa warned, speaking of Courtney's ex-fiancé that she'd left behind in the city when she'd been fired from her corporate marketing job.

"No. I just don't want to make any assumptions, and I know I have a lot going on with the shelter." Courtney reached down to pet Peppa, who seemed to be enjoying looking around just as much as Courtney was.

"So you're wanting to play it safe," Lisa concluded. "I get it, but a guy like Nathan isn't going to stay single for long. You don't want to miss out and regret it later."

Fortunately, a couple approached them just then. "Didn't we see you on the news?" the man asked. "From the shelter?"

"Yes, my name is Courtney Cain. Are you folks interested in adopting a pet?"

The woman looked up at her husband with excitement in her eyes. "We've been talking about it for a long time. I had a cat when I was a little girl, and she passed away before I went to college. We've always lived a pretty busy lifestyle, so we never felt like we had the time for a pet. It wouldn't be fair. But I saw the kittens that were on the other night, and I fell in love with the little tabby. Is she still available?"

"Oh, you're talking about Gingersnap. She's in her foster home at the moment with Shana, but she'll be ready for a home in about a week or so. I have some application forms in the car if you'd like one."

Soon enough, Courtney had run back to her car to get the paperwork to give to the Holts. They were so eager they sat down on a nearby bench and filled it all out immediately.

"When will know if we're approved?" Mrs. Holt asked. "I'm sorry to press. I'm just so worried that someone else will snap her up before we get the chance.

Courtney's heart reached out to her. Mrs. Holt hadn't even met Gingersnap in person yet, but she was already in love. Courtney hadn't worked at the shelter all that long, but she was getting an intuitive feel for people and pets who simply belonged together. "It should only be a day or two, and I'll make sure you're right at the top of Gingersnap's list. I could probably arrange for you to come meet her at the office one day next week if you like."

Mrs. Holt clapped her gloved hands together with glee. "Oh, that would be amazing! Thank you!"

"The work just never stops, does it?" Lisa asked when the Holts went off to check out the sleigh rides.

"Nope," Courtney agreed, "and neither does my work when it comes to the few bad things that happen in this town."

Lisa raised an eyebrow. "What is it this time?"

"You know how Reese Riley wanted to come to the shelter? Well, she did, and that Charlie Moss was supposed to be her cameraman."

"The grumpy one?" Lisa asked.

"That's the one," Courtney confirmed. "He never showed up, and when Reese called the studio to check on him, she found out he was dead."

"I assume you suspect foul play?" Lisa guessed.

"It's hard not to, considering the police have launched a full investigation. I tried calling Detective Fletcher, but he was busy. I'm not sure if I should conclude he was out shopping for Christmas presents or if he was investigating, but I'm pretty sure I know which one kept him from picking up."

The two of them strolled through the park, admiring the numerous smaller trees that had been decorated for the occasion. "Still, that doesn't sound like you have a lot of evidence to go off of."

"No evidence at all, really. I just know that something is up. While it's perfectly possibly for Charlie to have simply dropped dead, I feel like we would've heard something more about it by now. The news team themselves would probably report on it, mourning the loss of one of their own and all that. But I haven't heard a thing." Courtney stopped to let a little girl pet Peppa, taking a moment of joy in seeing how well the dog had adjusted to meeting new people.

When they'd moved on, Lisa picked the subject back up. "Do you have a list of suspects yet?"

"It's hard not to, considering how much tension there always was in the air down at the news studio. I can't believe how unprofessional everybody was. Charlie was certainly the heart of the problem, considering the way he insisted he was the only one who knew what he was doing. The first people on my list are the rest of the camera crew. You saw the way they reacted when Charlie insisted on being the one to head out and film that fire." Courtney had been mulling this over ever since she'd heard the news of Charlie's death.

"They were pretty upset," Lisa agreed as they paused to let two teenage boys run past. "I guess getting

Charlie out of the way would mean they'd have better chances at getting the big assignments."

Courtney nodded. "I imagine studio work is nice and steady, but it seems like a lot of folks in journalism are hoping to make a big break and be the next Tom Brokaw or Barbara Walters. We usually think of this in terms of the people who are on camera, but I'd be willing to bet it's the same for those behind the camera, too."

"In that case, could Reese Riley be a suspect?" Lisa speculated, keeping her voice low so it wouldn't carry through the cool air to anyone else in the park. For all they knew, the person who killed Charlie could be right there with them. "She was giving Charlie a lot of grief for the way the lighting was on the set and how it made her look. They were both pretty aggravated over it."

"I know." Courtney pulled her hat down a little further over her ears. It was getting colder, and she'd need to be heading home soon to make sure Peppa didn't get too chilly. "She mentioned to me how good the animals are for advancing her career, and she said something about looking for a job with another station. She's definitely looking to advance, and I could see how she might think Charlie was holding her back."

"That sounds like a really good lead." Lisa lifted her hand to wave to someone she recognized from the library.

"Yes, but I was with Reese when she heard the news about Charlie's death. She seemed genuinely shocked. I don't know how good of an actress she might be, but I felt like she really didn't have a clue until Mr. Holder told her over the phone." The high school band had started up 'Silent Night.' The trumpets and French horns rang clearly through the park, and Courtney made a mental note to support their next fundraiser. They were really quite good.

They made their way over to the souvenir booth, since Nathan had seemed to want her to, and Courtney bought a couple of mugs. It wasn't any more of a complicated transaction than it would've been if a stranger stood behind the table instead of Nathan, but Courtney had a hard time ignoring what Lisa had said earlier about Nathan possibly liking her. The whole thought made her feel like a teenager, and Courtney wasn't sure how to handle it.

"Anyone else?" Lisa asked as they turned toward the street where they'd parked.

"I thought about Kate Adams, who's in charge of all the charity work at the station. She was irritated with Reese more than anything, and she was concerned that she wouldn't get any of the credit for the shelter segments. I wondered if she might do something to frame Reese, but again I'm not going off of any proof." As they left the festivities behind, Courtney wondered how she was going to get to the bottom of this. She hadn't known any of these people until this week, and she didn't have any access to them now that the news spots were over. Once the shoot at the shelter had been cancelled due to Charlie's death, she hadn't heard a single word more.

"It could always be someone from his private life," Lisa pointed out. "Charlie wasn't well-liked at work, but for all we know he had a similar attitude when he was at home or out socially."

Courtney sighed as she fished in her coat pocket for her keys. "I know. That only makes it more difficult. Someone like Charlie probably had a lot of enemies, so how do you narrow it down?"

"You know, you could always take a little break from your sleuthing for the holidays and just let the police take care of it." Lisa pulled her own keys out of an inner zippered pocket, and Beau hopped on his front feet at the prospect of a car ride. "That's not as exciting, I know, but it might be a little less stressful for you."

"Yeah, right," she said with a smile. Courtney had hardly been able to cross anything off her numerous To-Do lists lately. "I mean, I've only got to continue promoting adoptions for the holidays, process all the adoption applications that the shelter has already received, return the forty or so phone calls that we missed, and do all my Christmas shopping. A little detective work on top of that is just a bit of icing on the cake, right?"

"Just don't work too hard," Lisa advised as she headed for her vehicle just a few yards away. "And call me if you need anything!"

Courtney and Peppa headed home. It was nice to see that the timer she'd set up on her Christmas tree had worked, and it was lit up and waiting for her in the front window when she got home. Next year, she'd put up some lights along the gutters and maybe decorate some of the bushes in the front yard, but for now it was a great start.

CHAPTER SEVEN

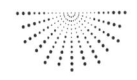

"Okay. I've left messages for everyone I didn't reach, so we may still get more people calling us back if they have any questions about the adoption applications. Flora, Autumn, Fishstick, and Scarlet each have a list of potential adopters about a mile long, so I think if anybody else calls about them we should say the waitlists are full. Same with Petunia's kittens." Courtney's head was spinning from trying to keep track of so many things. "Is your grooming schedule going all right for the holidays?"

Dora picked a bit of poodle fur off her shirt and dropped it in the trash can. "Busy as usual. Everyone has to have their pet looking perfect for all their holiday parties. I stocked up on lots of bows and hats and barrettes right around Thanksgiving, so I'm doing well."

"You're always so far ahead of the game. I envy and admire that," Courtney commented.

The groomer patted her shoulder. "You do better than you think you do. I only have one section of this place to run, and you're trying to hold down the entire fort. Don't forget that. What's this Holder guy wanting to see you about, anyway?"

"I don't know." Courtney's stomach had curled up inside her when Mr. Holder from down at News 5 had called her at work a few hours ago. "I thought at first he might be trying to reschedule the shoot here, but he just asked me to come into his office to talk. I guess I'll find out here in a few minutes."

"Don't worry about a thing. Jessi and I can take care of it all, and if we can't get to the phones on time, then the worst thing they can do is keep ringing." She winked and headed back into the salon, where an Afghan hound was waiting for its seasonal do.

Courtney really didn't have the time to take away from the shelter, despite Dora's reassurances. There was just always so much to do, and the holidays made that more complicated. The previous times she'd gone to the studio had at least been after-hours, but if this meeting with Mr. Holder was going to give them another chance to get more pets on the air, then she wasn't going to turn it down.

He was waiting for her in the front office when she arrived. "Ms. Cain! I almost didn't recognize you without one of your furry friends by your side. Thank you so much for coming, and on such short notice." Mr. Holder stepped forward to shake her hand.

"It's not a problem at all," she replied, even though that wasn't quite the truth. Mr. Holder was being a lot more pleasant than he had been in the other times she'd seen him, though of course he wasn't dealing with bad camera cables at the moment.

"Come on back to my office. Would you like a bottle of water? A cup of coffee?"

"Um, coffee would be fine, thank you."

"Joel! Two cups of coffee in my office right away!" Mr. Holder barked.

The young man who jumped at the command had bright blue eyes and curly hair. "Yes, sir!" he called back as he went running off.

Mr. Holder paused and waved Courtney in ahead of him. "Please, have a seat. Make yourself comfortable.

How's the weather going out there? Any snow flying yet?"

"No, not just yet. I hope there will be some for Christmas." Courtney sat in a hard plastic chair in front of Mr. Holder's desk. It filled her hair with static, and she brushed it forward over her shoulder so she wouldn't have to hear the crackle.

Joel came trotting in with a small plastic tray. Two News 5 coffee mugs full of dark liquid sloshed as he set them down. "Here you are, sir."

"Close the door on your way out, Joel."

The intern disappeared, and Courtney stirred a packet of sugar and a little cup of creamer into her mug.

"Now then," Mr. Holder began as he fixed his own coffee. "I first want to apologize to you for the way things have gone, both on your visits to the studio and when Ms. Riley came out to your workplace. We've had some issues among the staff, especially between Ms. Adams and Ms. Riley, and I'm working on fixing that to the best of my ability. It's not easy when you're dealing with people who all feel that the future of their careers relies on their daily performance."

"Doesn't it?" Courtney asked. "Pardon me for asking, but isn't that how they would get bigger jobs? By doing well here?"

He waved his hand impatiently through the air. "Oh, to a certain extent, but in the news business it's really more about chance. You have to be in the right place at the right time, and you can't be everywhere at once. To really make it big, you've got to luck into some amazing story that makes the whole world willing to glue their forehead to the television. No matter how good you are locally, it doesn't mean you're destined for a big break."

"I see." Courtney hadn't really thought about it like that. Then again, the most reporting she'd ever done only spanned a few small articles in her high school paper about the chess club championship and the new menu in the cafeteria.

"It's something I deal with every day, and I truly do apologize for everything you've experienced while you've been here. I brought you here today to say I hope we didn't scare you off. You see, the owner of the station wants us to make sure we focus on some sort of charity every holiday season. It's very good for our numbers, and it helps us make sure we remain relevant within the community. I have to say I wasn't expecting to do anything with animals this year, but it's a nice change and I don't want to try mixing it up too late in the season," Mr. Holder explained.

"I see. So you'd still like to do the shoot at the shelter?" Courtney asked hopefully. It would be a fantastic way to show as many of the animals as possible.

But the station manager shook his head. "I don't think it's the best idea. I'll spend far fewer of our resources if we keep everything here in the studio. I'd like—if you'd still be willing to do it—for you to bring in a few more rounds of adoptable pets as well as some of the people who have fostered or adopted. That helps put a little bit of variety in each segment, you see. I think the audience likes seeing the way these animals have impacted people, so I'm particularly interested in that part."

Courtney nodded. "I know for sure I can bring in more cats and dogs. I'd like for as many of them to get in front of the public eye as possible."

"Oh, I know what we can do!" Mr. Holder leaned forward and slapped his palm on the edge of the desk. "You email me some pictures of the pets. Dress them up for the holidays if you'd like. We can show a few of them every time we get ready to go to commercial break."

Courtney had felt uncertain when she'd first gotten the phone call from Mr. Holder, but she was starting to get really excited about this again. "Yeah, I can do that easily! We have pictures of most of them right now to post on our website anyway. And I'll make some calls and see if I can get anybody who's willing to come in and be on camera. That's the only part I'm worried about."

"Folks love being on camera, and they love being able to tell their friends and family to tune in and watch them. I'll bet you'll have more people lined up and ready to say yes than you know what to do with." Mr. Holder picked up his mug and took a big drink.

Courtney had nearly forgotten about her coffee up until now, and so she did the same. It was a little weak, but anything hot was nice this time of year. "I really do want you to know how much I appreciate the chance to use your station to find these dogs and cats new homes for the holidays. People sometimes forget how many unfortunate pets there are here in Curly Bay who are stuck in a cage instead of curled up on a coach or sleeping in front of the fire. We've already been getting more calls than we can handle on the pets that have been on the air so far."

"Good! I'm glad to hear it!" After another swig of coffee, Mr. Holder leaned forward and reached out to shake her hand. "Glad we can each help each other out like this."

Courtney finished her cup and stood up. "I'd better get going, as I have a few things I need to take care of before I can lock up for the day." She rested her hand on the doorknob without turning it, looking back over her shoulder at the station manager. "Since I'm here, I'd like to give you my condolences on the death of Charlie Moss."

The jovial look on Mr. Holder's face sagged a little. "Yes, thank you. That was very unexpected, and it's made a big impact on our team."

"Do you happen to know the funeral arrangements?" Courtney asked. It wasn't all right to ask if the death was suspicious, but this at least was socially acceptable.

Mr. Holder shook his head. "I don't think they've been made just yet."

"All right. Thanks, anyway. I'll call you as soon as I get some people lined up for interviews."

He winked. "You're wonderful, Ms. Cain!"

As she headed back out to her car, Courtney hoped she was doing the right thing. She knew that no matter what kind of issues the TV station had, the exposure was critical for their shelter. They couldn't get this type of publicity on their own without paying thousands of dollars in advertising fees, and that was money they needed to care for the pets. If she continued with the news segments and it went well enough, they could even empty the shelter by Christmas. Courtney had heard of such things happening in other places, but she'd never imagined it could transpire here in Curly Bay. The sheer number of phone calls they'd been getting, however, made Courtney really start to think it could be possible. She headed back home to the shelter, secretly hoping that on Christmas day, there wouldn't be a single animal left in those cages and kennels.

CHAPTER EIGHT

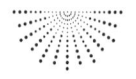

Courtney flipped to the next screen and dialed the number. "Hi, Carolyn! It's Courtney Cain. How are you doing today?"

"Courtney!" the realtor gushed. "I'm wonderful! How are you? Is everything going well with your house?"

Courtney had met Carolyn Davis initially when she was investigating the death of a local police officer. Subsequently, Carolyn had helped Courtney buy her house, and then she'd adopted a fluffy white cat named Coconut. Carolyn had a taste for fashion and home design, and she seemed like the perfect sort of woman who'd want a chance at being on television. "Oh, the house is wonderful! I've got it all decorated for the season, and it's just as perfect as I thought it would be. I was actually calling to see how you and Coconut are getting along, and to see if you might be interested in bringing her to the News 5 station for a segment they're doing about adopters." She made sure she smiled as she spoke. She'd always heard it made you sound friendlier over the phone.

"Coconut is absolutely wonderful, first of all," Carolyn replied. "I regret that I'm gone a lot, and I don't have as much time to spend with her as I like, but I make up for it when I'm at home. She is almost always on my lap, and at night she's usually sleeping right there on the bed with me."

"That's wonderful." Courtney could easily see how well Coconut would fit in with the pristine white interior of Carolyn's house.

"As for being on TV, I just don't have the time. You'd be surprised how much real estate is still moving while everyone is hanging garland."

Courtney raised her brows. "Really?"

"Oh, yes! People are very aware of the limitations of the current homes during the holidays. They realize they don't have enough room for out-of-town family, or they want a nicer background for their Christmas tree, or they simply decide a new home is the perfect gift for themselves. It happens all the time. Anyway, between work and the holiday I'm just too busy. Some other time, perhaps."

"I understand. I appreciate your time, and give Coconut a pet for me." Courtney hung up, feeling her whole body sag forward.

"That bad?" Jessi asked as she walked into the office with a whole new stack of adoption applications.

"Bad enough. Mr. Holder really wants to have fosters or adopters on the air. I can't blame him. It makes the story not just about the pets but about the people, and some folks might really respond to that. The problem is that everyone is either too busy or just doesn't want to be on TV." She clicked through to the next name on her list, knowing it was just going to be another disappointment.

"I can't say I blame them," Jessi said as she picked up the stack of mail on the corner of her desk and began flipping through it.

Courtney shrugged. "I know you're not interested, but Mr. Holder seemed so confident that I'd have tons of people wanting to do this. It makes me really worried that I'm going to let him down, and I can't risk him changing his mind on having us on the air." The phone rang again. "See?"

Jessi smiled and answered the phone. "Curly Bay Pet Hotel and Rescue. This is Jessi. How can I help you?" She cast a glance toward Courtney. "I'm afraid the waitlist for Scarlet is full, but we have quite a few other dogs available. You're welcome to come in and meet them. Can I schedule an appointment for you? Wonderful!"

At least they'd had one good boost from the news. Now it was Courtney's job to find a way to extend it. She next phoned the Wagners, a young couple who had become one of their best foster homes. "Hi, Allison! It's Courtney from the shelter. How are you guys?"

The sound of barking came through the line. "It's all right, Bravo. It's just the phone. See? Yes, that's a good boy. Sorry about that, Courtney."

"Not at all." The Wagners were so incredibly patient with any of the animals they brought home, and it meant the world to Courtney. They really needed fosters if they were going to take in every animal. "I just wanted to check in with you guys and see if you wanted to be on the news. They've been doing pieces about the animals we have here as well as the foster families, and I think you guys would be a great fit."

"Oh. Um, I appreciate the thought, but I don't think we're really interested."

"I know a lot of people are kind of shy about being on camera, but Reese Riley gave me some great tips that can really help. In fact, she really made me feel comfortable sitting there talking to her. It was like we weren't on TV at all, and it wouldn't be a long interview." Courtney was starting to feel desperate.

"No, thanks. It's not really anything like that. We've just heard some bad stuff about the TV station, and we don't want to get involved with any of that."

There was a long pause on the line as Courtney tried to figure out how to process this. "Can I ask what you heard?"

"Well," Allison hesitated. "One of their cameramen died recently, and I heard it wasn't just an accident or natural causes."

"I see." Courtney's heart was pounding in her chest. "So you think someone was killed?"

"We know someone who does a little bit of the sound work down at the station, and he said there was definitely foul play. He wouldn't say any more than that, but he's someone we really trust. He wouldn't make it up. Obviously I don't know anything concrete, and you know how rumors fly around a small town like this, but I do think it's suspicious. I'd rather just not have anything to do with that place. I hope you can understand, and normally there isn't anything we wouldn't do to help you guys out." Allison sounded truly worried over the phone.

"I do understand," Courtney responded. "Thanks for your honesty. I hope you guys have a Merry Christmas." She rang off and once again felt completely defeated. She couldn't find anyone to be on TV, and now she had yet another confirmation that someone had killed Charlie Moss.

Courtney closed out the window on her computer, but that meant she could see the one she'd opened earlier. She had started a spreadsheet of all the people she wanted to buy Christmas gifts for. All her family and friends were on there, but they only had their names listed. None of the gifts had been purchased yet. Further down on the sheet was another list of everything she wanted to do for the holidays, like send out cards and make cookies. The only one she'd managed to check off was putting up her tree. This was shaping up to be a very frustrating yuletide. Courtney closed the window and headed over to the shelter side.

She found Jessi just coming in the back door of the kennels with a very happy Flora on the end of a leash. "Whew! I'm glad I brought my hat today. It's really getting brisk out there. Not that the dogs mind." Jessi put Flora back in her kennel, unclipped the leash, and hung it on the wall.

"I've got a couple of questions for you, if you have a minute," Courtney began.

"Sure. Did you find anybody to do the next news bit for you?"

Courtney rolled her eyes and reached in through the chain link to scratch Scarlet's nose. "No, but that's exactly what I wanted to ask you about. You said your brother had interned at News 5. Does he still keep up with any of the office gossip over there?"

Jessi tipped her head to the side thoughtfully. "You know, I'm really not sure. He's got enough connections that he could pull the strings and get us the airtime, but beyond that I'm not sure."

"Do you think you could ask him?"

Now Jessi was really curious. "This has something to do with that cameraman's death, doesn't it? I knew it! If it was anything other than someone just having a heart attack, you'd be on the case!"

"I don't know anything for sure yet," Courtney reminded her. "But I do know that things were very tense down at the studio, as you saw. And just now on the phone, Allison Wagner said their sound guy told her it was probably foul play. It's all just hearsay, I know, but it's just reinforcing what I already thought was happening."

"I'll ask him," Jessi promised. "He's covering some big political scandal in the city right now, so it may be a bit before I can really talk to him about it, though."

"That's fine. Anything is better than nothing."

"What else did you want to ask me?"

Courtney pressed her hands together in front of her chest. She didn't want to feel hopeful about this, because she didn't want to get her hopes up and then see it all fall apart. "Has there ever been a time when there weren't any animals in the shelter?"

Jessi's reply was a laugh. "Not even when it was first opened, considering Ms. O'Donnell had already been taking dogs and cats into her home."

"Darn. That's what I figured. If we've never done it before, then I highly doubt we can do it now."

Courtney bit her lip, wishing she hadn't already gotten her hopes built up so high.

"What are you thinking?"

"Well, has the shelter ever been empty for Christmas?" Courtney dared to ask.

Jessi shook her head. "If you've got big plans for the day and you're worried about someone coming in to take care of all the animals, then it's no problem. I can come in early and take care of it. We don't start our big family celebration until later in the afternoon, anyway."

"It's not that. I just thought with all the phone calls we'd been getting, and the fact that we still have several more on-air spots before Christmas, that we might be able to find a home for everyone. Or at least a foster home, so they can wake up and share the day with some loving people. I know the dogs and cats don't really know it's a holiday, but I just thought it would be nice."

"It *is* nice," Jessi confirmed. "I can't say it's ever happened before, but that doesn't mean we can't try."

"First, I've just got to find someone else who's willing to go on TV. Then I guess I'll go from there."

Courtney started to head toward the office when Jessi touched her arm.

"Off subject, but there's a big sale on wrapping paper down at Pen and Paper, if you need to pick up a few extra rolls."

"I haven't even gotten my wrapping paper out yet," Courtney admitted. "I'm going to have some long nights ahead of me."

Back at her desk, she clicked to the next adopter and called Gerald Powell.

"Well, hey, Courtney!" His voice was bright and enthusiastic. "How are things going down at the shelter?"

She'd started off with some small talk when she called the other folks, but Courtney was really starting to feel the pressure of her limited time. "Not too bad. Hey, I don't know if you've seen the TV segments we've been doing on the news, but I was wondering if you might want to come to the studio and talk about Henderson."

"Really? Me? Well! How about that?" Gerald hadn't intended to adopt Henderson, but the big hound mix had continuously run away from his foster home and ended up on Gerald's front porch. The old man had taken the whole thing in stride, enjoying his first cup of coffee with the dog at his feet before bringing him back to the shelter. It didn't take long for him to figure out that the two of them were meant to be together.

"It would just be a short segment, just like you've seen us do so far. You'll bring Henderson in and talk to Reese Riley about adopting him and how your lives together are." She didn't want to once again inspire too much hope in herself, but Gerald sounded interested.

"Well, sure! I'd love to do that. I'll give the old boy a bath, and I might even iron my shirt!" he cackled.

"Wonderful! Thank you so much, Gerald. I'll confirm everything with the station manager, but most likely I'll be meeting you at the studio tomorrow night around five. Does that sound good?" She was smiling for the first time that day. It was just a small thing, but it'd really been weighing on her.

"What do you think, Henderson? Are you a good boy? Do you want to be on TV? You think they'll want to see you and those big brown eyes of yours? Yeah, I think so too!" Gerald laughed again, and it was easy to envision him ruffling the big dog's ears.

"Sure thing, Miss Courtney. I'll see you there tomorrow night unless I hear different from you."

When Courtney hung up, she took a moment to just absorb the warmth and joy of knowing that Henderson had found the person he was supposed to be with. Courtney wanted that for all the animals in the shelter, and all the animals in the world, really. But at least she knew that she'd helped as many of them as she could, and she would keep on trying.

CHAPTER NINE

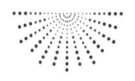

The next night, Courtney once again pulled into the parking lot in front of the station. She was starting to feel like being on the news was her second job, except of course that she didn't get paid for it. That was all right, because the sweet golden retriever mix in the seat next to her was probably going to get a new home in the next few days, thanks to being here. Courtney reached over to fix the Christmas collar she'd put on the dog for the occasion. "You're such a sweetheart, and everyone is going to fall all over themselves after they see you on the air," she said gently. "You're the type of dog everyone imagines themselves having, with their kids and their white picket fence. You might not be a puppy anymore, but you'll feel like you are when you're with your new family." That was the one 'problem' with Grace: she was four years old. There were so many people who didn't realize how nice it could be to skip the puppy phase.

Gerald and Henderson had also just arrived, and he parked next to her in his big truck. Henderson sat proudly in the passenger seat. Even though he wore his collar and leash, it was clear by the way he jumped out of the truck and stood next to his human that it was only for appearances. Henderson wasn't going to go anywhere unless Gerald asked him to. "Hello, ladies! It's a beautiful day!" Gerald beamed.

"I'm so glad you could do this for us, Mr. Powell," Courtney said. She'd already thanked him over the phone, but when she considered how hard it'd been to find anyone to fill this position, she was doubly grateful. "This is such a good promotion for the shelter."

"I understand," he replied as they headed for the door. "You've got to get yourselves out in front of people. I have to admit that even though I knew about the shelter, I never really thought about getting a dog until Henderson showed up. It was just the right timing and the right circumstances, but maybe it'll be that way for someone at home who happens to see that beautiful girl you've got there." He pointed to Gracie.

The golden girl looked a little uncertain, but not scared as she looked around. "I think so, too. It's been like a Black Friday sale for the other dogs and cats that we've already brought in, with people practically lining up at the door to adopt. I can only wish that it was like that all the time, but I'll take what I can get."

They moved through the office and into the studio itself, where Gerald gave a low whistle. "Look at all this stuff," he said as he took in the thick bundles of cables on the floor and the microphones that hung down from the ceiling. "And all just so they can read the news. That's something else."

A high whine made Courtney looked quickly down at Grace. She'd picked the dog for the next segment because of her sweet disposition. They'd had her around other dogs, as well as cats, and she'd never had a problem. She greeted strangers with a wagging tail and sometimes even a lick on the back of the hand. But something was bothering her right now. She danced from side to side with her ears pinned back, whining and fussing.

"What's wrong with her?" Gerald asked, frowning in concern. Henderson was wagging his tail and sniffing at a nearby tripod.

"I'm not sure. I guess there's a limit to everyone's patience." Knowing that she had Gerald and Henderson booked for the evening had relieved the vast majority of Courtney's stress. Sure, she still had plenty of Christmas preparations to take care of, but this was far more important. Seeing the way Gracie was reacting wasn't a good start to the evening. She knelt down, stroked Gracie's back, and whispered to her soothingly in the hope of calming her.

It wasn't working. By the time Mr. Holder came out to see if they needed anything, Gracie had worked herself up even more. She was growling and barking, pulling at her leash as though she was trying to get away.

"What's wrong with her?" he asked, pointing at the dog with the file folder in his hand.

Gracie jumped backwards as though he was going to hit her.

"I think she's just freaking out a little," Courtney admitted. They almost never had a dog at the shelter that she couldn't handle. Some of them were scared or shy, but they didn't do anything to really make

Courtney feel as if they were out of control. "I'm sorry. I'm not sure what's wrong."

"We can't have that," Mr. Holder said, gesturing with the file and scaring Gracie all over again. "We'll be going on the air in just a few minutes. Why don't you take her into my office? We'll put Mr. Powell on first, and if she hasn't calmed down by then, we'll keep it to just these two." He smiled approvingly at Henderson, who had sat down next to Gerald and was whipping his tail with enthusiasm.

"Thank you. I'll do that. Gerald, I should introduce you to Miss Riley really quick and show you around." The other trips to the studio hadn't turned out the way she wanted them to, but on those times it hadn't been her fault. The fact that it was one of her shelter dogs who was causing the current ruckus made Courtney extremely uncomfortable.

But the station manager was eager to get the noisy, scared dog out of the way. "I'll take care of all that, Courtney. Just have a seat, and I'll come check on you once Mr. Powell is on the air."

She felt so torn. It didn't feel right to have invited Gerald here and then basically abandon him. But the old man was looking around with interest and enthusiasm, and he didn't seem bothered in the least about being handed over to a stranger. Maybe she needed to give him more credit. "All right. Thank you. And I'm sorry."

Courtney headed over to the same office where she'd met with Mr. Holder earlier in the week and shut the door behind her. She sat down and patted her knee. "It's all right, Gracie. I promise. I know this is a strange place for you, and it might seem even scarier than a shelter. All the smells and people are different. At least we don't have everyone fighting today. That would've been much worse, I promise."

Now that she said it, Courtney realized just how much more pleasant the studio had been. Nobody had been fighting or arguing, and as far as she could tell everything was flowing along the way it was supposed to. Had Charlie's death changed that because he wasn't there to antagonize everybody? Or were all the staff in mourning? It was hard to say.

Unfortunately, getting away from the studio hadn't done Gracie any favors. She refused to pay any attention to Courtney's efforts. She jerked against her leash as she paced the office, lunging first toward the door, then back to the desk. She even stood up on her hind legs to try to look out the window.

"Oh, honey. I'm so sorry. You want a treat?" Courtney had stowed a few in her pocket, and she held one out.

Gracie barely even gave it a cursory sniff before she was dashing around the room again, sniffing under the desk and trying to get underneath Courtney's chair.

A small TV monitor had been mounted to the wall, and it showed the live news broadcast that was happening in the other room. Courtney brought Gracie close and stroked her fur as she watched. The volume was mostly turned down, but she could see Reese smiling beautifully at the camera as she talked about what a success the tree lighting ceremony was and reminded viewers that the local coat and hat drive was still going on.

Now that the dog was a little more settled, Courtney started thinking once again about Charlie Moss. Allison Wagner said her friend insisted there was foul play. Courtney hadn't been able to reach Detective Fletcher, which was odd. He was usually happy to let her in on a little bit of knowledge, considering how much she helped him out. That certainly made Courtney wonder just how busy he might be on this case. Considering that Charlie was associated with the local news station, Fletcher might be taking extra precautions to keep it under wraps.

She rubbed her teeth against her bottom lip, thinking about her list of suspects. All of them worked here at the station. Kate Adams obviously had some animosity toward her coworkers. Charlie's fellow cameramen certainly didn't appreciate him. Reese Riley felt she had a lot to gain in her career, and yet Charlie was holding her back.

It wasn't the type of thing she'd normally do, but Courtney knew she had the opportunity of a lifetime while she was here in Mr. Holder's office. The broadcast on the monitor told her she still had some time before Gerald Powell would go on the air. She moved around behind Mr. Holder's desk.

Courtney expected the drawers to be locked, but the first one she tried slid open easily. It was full of numerous station pens, a messy stack of business cards, and a tangled mess of paperclips. Not very interesting.

The drawer underneath it was full of file folders. Courtney flicked through the tabs, reading each one carefully with Gracie at her side. Most of them seemed all just a normal part of the news business, regarding sponsors, charities they'd helped in the past, and correspondence from his boss. Further behind, she realized she'd found the files for each employee. Courtney's heart thundered in her chest as she found a rather thick folder on Reese Riley.

The most recent information had been put in on top of the rest, detailing a few instances between Reese and her coworkers. These went back all the way to when Reese had first been hired, and plenty of them were between her and Charlie. There were also a few between Reese and Kate, arguing about who should take either the credit or the responsibility for something. To Courtney, it all looked like overly dramatic stuff that should've been left behind in school.

Kate Adams had a file, as well. It seemed Mr. Holder thought she'd done a great job hosting a blood drive and getting various charities on the air. But there was a stack of complains in here as well. Some of these were simply copies of the ones in Reese's file, but Courtney noted several involved Charlie. One memo said Kate recommended Charlie be fired for showing up drunk. Another was a complaint about the way Charlie cursed while in the studio, no matter who was around.

It was all very interesting, but the one file she really wanted was just behind it. Charlie Moss. Courtney pulled it out, expecting it to be the thickest one yet. Instead, it was incredibly thin. There was Charlie's original application stapled to the inside, topped with a few notes about raises and promotions.

"That's it?" Courtney whispered to Gracie. "Why aren't any of the complaints in his file?"

Her phone buzzed, and she impatiently fished it out of her pocket. She had to get this finished and get out of here. But Jessi was calling, and if by any chance there was something wrong at the shelter or with one of their foster pets, she'd never forgive herself if she didn't answer. "Hey, what's up?" she whispered.

"I'm sorry. I know you're busy. I just wanted to let you know I talked with Jason."

"Who? Oh! Sorry. I'm a little distracted." Courtney flicked through the remainder of Charlie's file, wondering why she didn't see a scrap of disciplinary action on the man. It was no wonder he'd continued to act up when he was constantly getting away with it. Courtney set the file down on the top of Mr. Holder's desk and checked the drawer, wondering if perhaps there was a secondary file that contained all of Charlie's demerits. He certainly seemed to be deserving of one.

"That's okay. I talked to Jason and I told him about Charlie Moss. He said he really wasn't surprised. The man has been at the station forever, and he wasn't liked back when Jason worked there, either."

"Well, that's nothing new." Courtney glanced up at the monitor. They were heading into the weather report, which meant Mr. Powell and Henderson would be on soon. She was running out of time.

"No, but he also told me that Charlie Moss is related to the station manager by marriage. He hired him years ago as a favor to his wife. Charlie is his wife's cousin, and he'd lost his job at one of the big stations. Nobody else would hire him, so Mr. Holder did. But now he can't fire him, or else he'll make his wife angry."

Courtney slowly stood up. She looked down at the file with Charlie's name on it that she'd set on the desk. "That all makes sense," she said quietly. "Nobody liked him. Charlie was constantly causing trouble with everyone else, and yet Mr. Holder only made excuses for him or ignored the problem completely. That also explains why he never got a write-up." She swallowed, though her mouth felt suddenly dry. "I need to go, Jessi. But I'll talk to you soon."

Just as she hung up, the office door swung open. "Hey, Courtney. How's the dog—what are you doing?" He froze in the doorway as he observed Courtney standing behind his desk with the drawers open and a file out.

"I can explain," she said quickly.

Gracie bared her teeth, growling at Mr. Holder. She'd been mostly fine a moment ago, but she had her hackles up all over again at his arrival. Courtney couldn't blame her.

Mr. Holder crossed his arms in front of his chest, blocking the doorway with his bulk. "Well, it'd better be a good one, and you'd better shut that dog up!"

"I'll do no such thing," Courtney asserted. Her initial reaction when she'd been caught was to make an excuse as to why she was spying on Mr. Holder, and even though she'd been snooping, she wasn't really the one in the wrong here. "And if anyone has an explanation to give, it's you!"

"What do you mean?" he snarled, his dark eyes glaring.

But Courtney noticed the beads of sweat running down his temples. He usually got his feathers up during the broadcast, but he was nervous. "You know what happened to Charlie Moss," she said, tapping her finger on the file.

Mr. Holder took two steps forward through the little office and swiped the file off the desk. "He's dead. Everyone knows that. What's your point?"

Gracie's growl turned deeper and more serious now that Mr. Holder was closer, and she made sure to position herself between the station manager and Courtney.

"My point is that you killed him. You hired him because he was related to your wife, but you never expected him to be so much trouble. You couldn't fire him, so you found a different way to get him out of your studio."

Mr. Holder's mouth moved like he was trying to chew a giant bite of Christmas ham. "You're worse than all these reporters I work with, constantly looking for a story where there isn't one. I'll thank you to get out of my office and keep your wild theories to yourself."

"I'll get out," Courtney promised, "but I'm not leaving this alone. I know what happened, and I might not have much evidence, but I'll find it." She started for the door.

"I don't think so." Mr. Holder lunged to the side to stop her.

Gracie leapt up between the two people, putting her paws on Mr. Holder's chest and shoving him backward. He fell to the floor, slamming his elbow on the open door and sending it shivering against the wall. The dog was determined, standing over him and barking as loud as she could. Mr. Holder rolled over onto his stomach and got up onto his hands and knees, crawling through the door in an effort to get away from the big dog.

Unfortunately, Gracie only saw this as an opportunity. She opened her jaws wide and planted her teeth right into Mr. Holder's backside.

The three of them burst into the studio, right in the middle of the broadcast. Mr. Holder was on his feet now, screaming unintelligibly as he scrambled over all the cables on the floor. He managed to make it onto the stage, running directly in front of the cameras in the middle of the newscast as Reese Riley interviewed Mr. Powell. Gracie was directly behind him, snapping at the back of his pants.

Kate Adams burst out of the control room. "What's going on?"

"Call the police! That man killed Charlie Moss!" Courtney said.

Reese Riley cleared her throat and looked into the camera. "That's all we have for you tonight, folks, but stay tuned tomorrow for more details. Have a great evening."

CHAPTER TEN

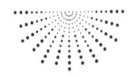

"This is quite the party!" Kate Adams said as she walked into the lobby of the Curly Bay Pet Hotel and Rescue. "Should we have come at another time?"

"Not at all," Courtney assured her. "We're not just celebrating Christmas here. We've had tons of adoption applications put in over the last few weeks, and we've got plenty of fosters and adopters who are coming in today to take their new fur friends home. I haven't stopped smiling all day!" It might not be a traditional Christmas Eve, but it was certainly one that made her happy.

Reese Riley, who'd come in with Kate, held her hands clasped in front of her chest. "And you said my application was approved?" she asked hopefully.

"Absolutely. Here's your little guy right here." Courtney had Carrot all ready to go, with a big plaid bow around his neck.

"Oh, hello, sweet thing!" Reese snuggled the little orange cat, rubbing her chin on his head. "We're going to have the best Christmas ever, aren't we? Yes, we are!"

Joel, the intern from the station, had come along with them as well. He watched the anchorwoman for a moment before he looked at Courtney shyly. "I just wanted to see if my application was approved."

"Oh, yes. I wanted to talk to you about that for a second. Come over here." Courtney brought him back to the office area and to her desk. They passed the Holts on the way, who were fawning over Gingersnap. When they were mostly alone, she sat Joel down at her desk. "I had no problem approving your application, but I wanted to talk to you about Gracie. Though she was only doing what her instincts told her to, biting Mr. Holder got her into a bit of trouble."

"But he's a killer!" Joel argued.

"Yes, I know. It might not be a big deal except that she did it right on TV," Courtney continued. The incident had turned out for the best, as Gracie had both stopped Mr. Holder from doing anything to harm Courtney and from leaving the station. Joel spent some time with her while they waited for the police to come, and when Courtney went to fetch her she found the dog asleep in the intern's lap. "I can let you adopt her, but you have to agree to take her to some training classes to make sure she doesn't develop any bad habits. There's a trainer by the name of Shawn Ryder who's really great."

Joel nodded immediately. "Absolutely. Not a problem."

Courtney appreciated his eagerness, but there was something she needed to know. "Are you adopting Gracie just because you saw her put your boss in his place?" she asked quietly.

"No. I can see why you would ask, since Mr. Holder yelled at me all the time, but no. I saw all those poor animals you brought in, and I felt really bad for them. At first, I didn't think it was really a problem I could do anything about. After I spent some time with Gracie, though, I realized how much she really needed someone. She's a sweet dog, and I don't like thinking about her being in a shelter. No offense to you," he quickly added.

"None taken at all. Just sign here and here for me." She pushed two papers across the desk for Joel.

"There you are, Courtney!" It was Mrs. Throgmorton, one of the best clients the hotel and day spa could ever have hoped for. She often helped with big fundraising events, as well. "I just got back from my ski trip in Aspen, and I heard about all the drama on the news. I take it by the looks of this party that everything is back to rights?"

"Oh, and then some," Courtney said with a smile. "We're getting ready to head over to the kennel side. You should come with us." She got up from her desk and went through the door to the shelter side.

It was incredibly quiet. Most of the cage doors stood open, and the name tags next to them had been taken down. "What's going on?" Mrs. Throgmorton asked as they passed the cat room and into the kennel.

"As you heard, we were on the news quite a bit. The individual cats and dogs we featured were very popular, and we had tons of people who wanted to adopt them. Most of them ended up coming in and seeing the other animals instead, and that adoption boom only got bigger after Gracie here caught a killer right on camera." Courtney opened Gracie's cage and stood to the side.

The dog came bursting out of her kennel and straight into Joel's arms, her fur flying and her tongue flapping. She practically knocked him into the opposite wall, but he didn't care. Joel wrapped his arms around her and laughed while she covered his face in kisses. "Hi, Gracie! Yes! I'm glad to see you, too!"

"I'm just glad Gracie didn't end up with a bad rap. Biting someone on live TV probably isn't the best idea for a dog, but Reese Riley did a full report on the escapade the very next night and painted her to be the hero she was. Since then, we've had to stay open late just to get everything processed. By the time everyone leaves tonight, there won't be a single cage filled." Courtney watched Gracie and her new owner together, knowing she wouldn't need to worry about Gracie or Carrot or Scarlet or any of the other animals this Christmas season. It would truly be a silent night in the shelter, as everyone was home for the holidays.

Mrs. Throgmorton hugged her. "I'm so glad to hear it, Courtney. That sounds like a news story in and of itself."

"It is," Courtney agreed, "and it's the best Christmas present I ever could've asked for."

THANK YOU FOR CHOOSING A PUREREAD BOOK!

We hope you enjoyed the story, and as a way to thank you for choosing PureRead we'd like to send you this free Special Edition Cozy, and other fun reader rewards…

Click Here to download your free Cozy Mystery
PureRead.com/cozy

Thanks again for reading.
See you soon!

OTHER BOOKS IN THIS SERIES

The Missing Pom Mystery

The Case of the Confused Canine

A Case Full of Cats

A Furry case of Foul Play

The Case of a Beagle and a Body

A Case of Canines, Cats, & Costumes

A Case of Frauds and Friendly Lizards

A Very Furry Christmas Mystery

The Mysterious Case of Books, Barks, & Burglary

Also, be sure to get your free copy of Sunny Cove Sleuths

PureRead.com/cozy

OUR GIFT TO YOU

AS A WAY TO SAY THANK YOU WE WOULD LOVE TO SEND YOU THIS SPECIAL EDITION COZY MYSTERY FREE OF CHARGE.

Our Reader List is 100% FREE

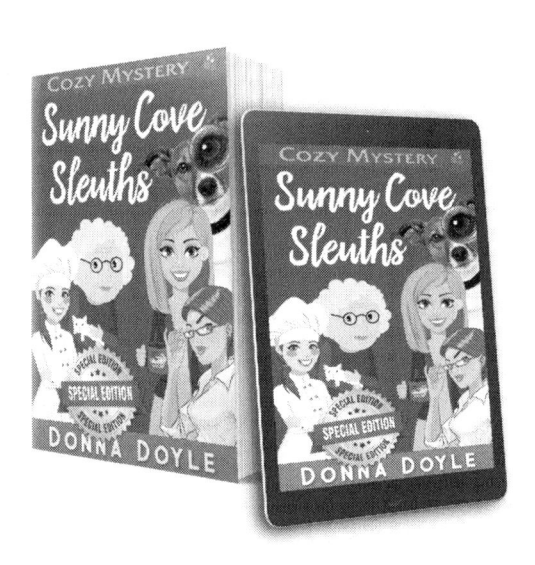

Click Here to download your free Cozy Mystery
PureRead.com/cozy

At PureRead we publish books you can trust. Great tales without smut or swearing, but with all of the mystery and romance you expect from a great story.

Be the first to know when we release new books, take part in our fun competitions, and get surprise free books in your inbox by signing up to our Reader list.

As a thank you you'll receive this exclusive Special Edition Cozy available only to our subscribers...

Click Here to download your free Cozy Mystery
PureRead.com/cozy

Thanks again for reading.
See you soon!